Marvin Richardson Vincent

Christ as a Teacher

Marvin Richardson Vincent

Christ as a Teacher

ISBN/EAN: 9783742811288

Manufactured in Europe, USA, Canada, Australia, Japa

Cover: Foto ©Andreas Hilbeck / pixelio.de

Manufactured and distributed by brebook publishing software
(www.brebook.com)

Marvin Richardson Vincent

Christ as a Teacher

CHRIST AS A TEACHER.

TWO LECTURES

DELIVERED BEFORE THE NEW YORK SUNDAY-SCHOOL
TEACHERS' ASSOCIATION.

BY

MARVIN R. VINCENT, D.D.

NEW YORK:

ANSON D. F. RANDOLPH & COMPANY,

900 BROADWAY, COR. 20th STREET.

EDWARD O. JENKINS' SONS,
Printers and Stereotypers,
20 North William St., New York.

CHRIST AS A TEACHER.

I.

IT is a vast and most tempting subject which you have assigned me. At best you will not expect me to do more than to touch a point here and there on the circumference of the theme. That I may do even thus much, let me waste no time in preliminary words. I am to speak of CHRIST AS A TEACHER.

None of us will dispute the rightfulness of the title which our Lord gives Himself in the thirteenth of John (v. 13): "Ye call me *master* (or teacher) and Lord, and ye say well, for so I am." He is the representative teacher; the teacher of teachers; the model and the inspiration of the most successful theories of teaching. Back to Him we must go, down the whole long line of sages and philosophers, for the best example of the art of expounding truth to uninstructed minds. Our admiration grows as we apprehend the conditions under which He taught, and the character of His material. He had not to deal with virgin soil.

The teacher who grapples with a fresh mind, unbiased by religious opinions or definite religious conceptions, has a great advantage over one who must reach a mind through a jungle of *false* conceptions and prejudices, rooted in tradition, developed by false methods of training, and backed by perhaps the most arrogant and dictatorial ecclesiasticism the world has ever known. It was very much for even *some* such auditors to say, "Never man spake like this man."

THE POWER OF CHRIST'S PERSONALITY.

And here we catch more than a hint of the first great element of Christ's power as a teacher—HIS PERSONALITY. It was the *man* that carried and drove home the teaching.

Power in teaching is bound up with character in the teacher. Truth, from a real teacher, is not like water running through a marble or silver channel which imparts no character to it. It is rather like water in a medicated cup which communicates its flavor to the liquid. A mind is not merely a receptacle for facts; it is a germ to be *informed*, and only life can inform with life. Formulas of truth quicken as the teacher's life pervades them. The instinct of the youngest pupil is to put the teacher before the lesson. Scores of men who never exerted a fraction of Thomas Arnold's power over English youth, were his superiors in knowledge and in what goes to make the drill-master ; but the best thing which the Rugby boys carried away from Rugby was the impress of Arnold himself.

The great illustration of this truth is Christ. The power of Christianity is the power of a *person* rather than of a *system*. His words are " spirit and life," because He speaks them. I do not mean merely that His presence was commanding and His mode of speech fascinating, though that might well be the case ; but I mean that the Man and His sayings were inseparably welded ; that the sayings were the outcome of the man's inmost quality and fibre. Christ is the incarnated denial of the French diplomatist's falsehood that " the great object of language is to conceal thought." Christ himself appeared through all the windows of His speech. You would not be slow to appreciate the difference between Webster's reply to Hayne, thundered forth by the great expounder of the Constitution in person, and the same speech declaimed in the best style by a clever school-boy. You do not stop to analyze such differences ; you feel them. Of Christ it has been beautifully said, " To hear His daily speech was not simply to receive His thoughts but to share, as it were, the inmost life of His spirit. His speech is, after eighteen centuries, exceeding wonderful to the world, and humanity still listens to it as one listens to a tale he can not choose but hear; yet to the men who first heard it, it was made fully intelligible by His person. To hear His speech was to enjoy His fellowship; and His fellowship created the sense that understood His speech. His words came to them explained by a living and articulate commentary." That was pre-eminently true of our Lord which was said of a certain literary character of England, that "his conversation was companionship and his companionship conversation." Christ's words, spoken by Plato or Aristotle, would not have been "spirit and life." No homily or treatise will generate the enthusiasm of a true student. Men will not suffer martyrdom for an abstraction, nor meet a code with self-surrender. Self will not capitulate to sermons. The sermon must flame into a life. Christ at the tomb of Lazarus gives the real clench to Paul's argument in First Corinthians: "Love your enemies" must be translated into the wood and nails of the cross before men will decipher it.

The first and highest requisite of a Sunday-school teacher, therefore, is a well-defined Christian personality. Study of the Scriptures will not, of itself, make a teacher. The work begins deeper than that. The teacher is not set merely to explain the geography and the customs of Bible lands or the meaning of hard texts. He is not merely to give his pupils information : he is to inform them with the quality of a Christ-like character ; and for this he must have "Christ formed within" him. He is to be a moral and spiritual power, not an encyclopædia. He is to be not mere ammunition, but powder on fire. Paul, as you remember, in his counsel to Timothy, puts self before teaching : "Take heed to *thyself* and unto thy teaching "; for it is thyself that teaches. Similarly he said to the Ephesian elders : "Take heed unto *yourselves* and unto the flock."

This whole line of thought will find further illustration in the second characteristic of our Lord's teaching, to which we now come.

CHRIST A DOGMATIC TEACHER.

Christ was a dogmatic teacher. I know that the word "dogma" jars upon some cars, but it is a fair question whether the word or the ear is responsible for the jar. A defective ear courts false harmonics. The King of Siam,

according to the story, was more delighted
with the orchestra's preliminary jargon in tun-
ing their instruments than with their grandest
symphony, and asked to have "that first piece"
repeated. Many are afraid of the word "dogma" because they mistake, or only partially
apprehend, its meaning. "Dogma" is a good
New Testament word, which always carries the
sense of authority. That was the very thing
which astonished the people in Christ's teaching. "He taught them as one having authority."
Possibly we believe in dogma more than we
think. If we follow back some of the things
about which we are surest, we may find that
they rest on dogma after all. You and I began
our education with dogma. When you stood
beside your mother and began upon the alphabet, little knew or cared you about Cadmus or
the theory of phonetics. Your mother said,
"That is A," and you believed it, and have
acted upon your belief ever since. I know
there is said to have been at least one excep-
tion to that rule. I have somewhere read of
a stuttering Block Island boy who essayed the
alphabet for the first time, and on being told
that the character on the blackboard was A,
replied, "H-h-how do y-you know i-it's A?"
The teacher meekly replied that her teacher
had told her so; whereupon the young skep-

tic, after a long look at the doubtful character, stolidly responded, "*H-h-how did you k-n-now he d-d-didn't l-l-lie?*" But we may safely affirm that such hopeless exceptions are rare. Most of us learned the alphabet dogmatically at our mother's knee or—over it. It was the same with the multiplication table, and with a hundred other things. We have no better reason for believing them than that we were told so. The purest dogmatism is the basis of at least two-thirds of our knowledge. Dogma is a fundamental necessity of our education. It is simply impossible, as it would be foolish if it were possible, to follow down every item of our knowledge to its roots. A life might be consumed upon a single item. It is at once our right and our duty to enter into other men's labors, and to stand upon the foundations they have laid. All honest and thorough work saves the time and the labor of future generations. No locomotive-builder thinks it necessary, in order to construct a perfect machine, that he should begin where Stephenson did, and work up through each successive stage to the present level of knowledge and mechanical skill. He starts with the latest and best model he can find.

No one will understand me to depreciate research, nor to mean that religious truth is to be received on mere authority, an idea which is contrary to the whole spirit, attitude, and teaching of the Gospel. It is a Christian apostle who bids us be ready to give to every man that asketh us a reason of the hope that is within us. But I am speaking of teaching and of methods of teaching; and my point is that all teaching must include dogma, and, ordinarily, must begin with dogma. If you want to instruct a child or an ignorant person about the soul, you do not begin with a discussion of the nature of spirit and matter; you do not pretend to lead the pupil through every stage of knowledge and proof. You start with dogmatic statement: "You have a soul, and that something in you which you know and feel is there,—that something which is not your hand nor your foot, nor anything about your body, but which thinks and wills and chooses, and is glad or sorry,—is your soul." I say dogma does not exclude question or research. On the contrary the true teacher dogmatizes in order to set his pupil thinking and asking questions. Properly viewed, dogma is the true preparation and stimulant for research.

Now, Christ's teaching is a notable illustration of this. Not that He does not invite question; not that He does not explain; but

the great, fundamental characteristic of His
method is *assertion*,—simple, authoritative
statement. "The facts about God and His
kingdom, and life and death and judgment,
are thus and so." And these statements were
not authoritative in form and manner only.
They carried the sense of authority, and im-
pressed and moved men from a point deeper
than their logic. Christ was a notable illustration of the remark that "power of statement is power of argument." Christ knew
men too well to attempt to reach the masses
with argument. Even the learned Nicodemus'
first essay is met with that most tremendous
dogma in the New Testament, "Except a
man be born again, he can not see the kingdom of God."

Perhaps we do not fully realize what a deli-
cate and dangerous experiment it was for a
radical reformer like Jesus,—a teacher of a
strange and unpopular doctrine,—to throw
Himself so much upon simple assertion. And
here comes in that power of Christ's personality already alluded to. It needed a wonderful
self to carry those assertions; it needed the
peculiar quality of that self infused into those
assertions so as to give them a self-evidencing
power. It is not every one that can dogmatize effectively. The power of a dogma lies

very much in who propounds it. When a youthful pulpit orator, fresh from the seminary, lays down the principles of family government to a congregation of fathers and mothers, all that he says may be thoroughly true, but the fathers and mothers either smile, or are thinking of something else; and the washerwoman in the corner under the gallery, with half a dozen rampant olive-plants at home, if she does not say as much, feels that she can tell the preacher a great deal more about his subject than he is telling her. The lesson, however truthful, is truth outside of the preacher, not a part of him; not the expression of experience or sympathy or anything residing in him. Therefore, the more dogmatic he is, the more absurd he is. It is simply stage-thunder. As the best-made cannon-ball is useless until fitted to its cannon, so the soundest and most compact dogma is impotent until it is cast in the mould of individual experience and propelled by personality.

Therefore Christ could dogmatize effectively. No one but Christ could have given lodgment to such words as—"Ye must be born again": "He that believeth not is condemned already": "God is a Spirit, and they that worship Him must worship Him in spirit and in truth": "He that loveth his life loseth it ": "On these two commandments hang all the law and the prophets." Back of all lay His deep, divine self-consciousness, the knowledge that He was Himself the Truth. When He taught, it was the Truth speaking the truth. No doubt lingered in any remote depth of His soul: no secret apprehension or haunting sense of possibility that any word of man could overthrow the word of the living God. Pure, absolute certainty was the fountain-head of His speech : intuitive certainty that what He uttered was the eternal verity and reality, beside which the imaginings and dialectic subtleties of worldly-wise men were but cobwebs. " He was certain that though He never wrote, only spoke, His words were imperishable, and would outlast heaven and earth. He was at the first as at the last certain of the reality of His words and claims, of their endurance and triumph. He was as calmly and consciously confident when He sat, pitied by Pilate, in the shadow of Calvary, as when He went forth, approved by John, to preach, in His fresh and glorious manhood, the Gospel of the kingdom of God."

Out of this we may draw at least one valuable practical lesson for the Christian teacher. There are indeed questions raised by the Gospel toward which he must bear himself as a humble and reverent learner. He comes, not unfrequently, to a something tangled and complicated to his human sense, like the bush on Horeb, yet like that bush, burning with God's fire, before which he can only stand with unshod feet, waiting for the voice from the flame. But the Gospel has certainties as well as mysteries. It would not be a Gospel else. And toward its great, fundamental positions, his attitude is to be that of *assurance*. In modern teaching there is often manifest too strong a disposition to put Christianity on the defensive. It was Coleridge, I believe, who declared that he was "sick of evidences of Christianity." We can not work for men's salvation with anything less than a certainty, held by us as it was held and propounded by Christ, as a fixed, unalterable, eternal fact. Men can not be moved to self-abandonment and self-consecration by an open question. If the Gospel is something yet to be proved, it is time that Christians, at least, abandoned it for something else. I know that Christianity involves questions which are yet in court; but none of these are vital. If, however, the Gospel itself is still a thing in doubt; if there is a possibility that science may yet put us out in the cold, without a Saviour and bankrupt in faith, and shivering in the blasts from every point of the philosophic compass,—I, for one, want no more of it. Let me go down from the Christian teacher's place, if my business there is only to urge a probability, or to flaunt a flag from the top of pasteboard bastions which the next shot from a well-trained infidel battery will breach. The alternative for us is a sure Gospel or no gospel. Evidences of Christianity have their function, and an important function ; but it is, I am inclined to think, in the majority of cases, rather the education of believers than the conviction of unbelievers. As Christian teachers our business is less to argue than to assert the Word of God, and the Gospel of Christ as the power of God unto salvation. A great modern preacher has well said, "If we would trust Christ's cross to stand firm without our stays, and, arguing less about it, would seldomer try to prop it and oftener to point to it, it would draw more men to it."

Sunday-school teachers must, in the nature of the case, be mostly dogmatic. "The creed of childhood," one has justly said, "must necessarily be imparted dogmatically." It must rest on authority ; and authority which carries home the truth to a child's mind is born of a living Christian personality in the teacher. The standard of preparation must not be let down; the demands of Scriptural study must be strictly met; but the carefully gathered knowledge, in order to move and impress the pupil, must be fused by the Holy Spirit into the mould of a living experience. In Bible-classes of older pupils, the teacher must, of course, be prepared to answer objections and to deal with doubts; but he must never take the attitude of a doubter himself. If a question is asked which he can not answer, or a problem raised which he can not solve (and the veriest child will often propound such), let him say so frankly, but always in such a way as to let it be understood that no possible solution or answer can in any wise disturb for him the solid groundwork and substance of the Gospel. He must never tread gingerly on Gospel ground. It is holy ground, but firm ground; and though he may not be able to arrange and explain all that is *upon* it, he is to step as one who knows that the Rock of Ages is *under* it.

CHRIST A SYSTEMATIC TEACHER.

I go on to note that Christ was a systematic teacher. I do not mean in the scholastic sense of elaborating a system of morals or theology. He left that for others. But it is a great mistake to suppose, as not a few do, that Christ's teaching was a disorderly collection of fragments which it should be the task of future students to sift out and arrange. Christ's teaching was methodical in its inner structure. This opens a very wide subject, and I can only touch a point here and there.

Take, for example, the progression in His teaching. Compare the last chapters of John's gospel with the Synoptists. A great advance is perceptible. The teaching is less rudimentary. It appeals to a higher grade of spiritual development. Transfer it to the beginning of Christ's ministry, and you at once perceive that it does not fit there. "The Sermon on the Mount at the opening of the ministry, and the address in the upper chamber delivered at its close, are separated from each other, not only by difference of circumstance and feeling, but as implying on the part of the hearers wholly different stages in the knowledge of truth."* Matthew throws a

---

* Thomas Dehany Bernard, "The Progress of Doctrine in the New Testament." This most valuable and suggestive book, of which a cheap American Edition has been published, ought to be on the desk of every Bible-class teacher. On this topic the teacher may also profitably consult Canon Westcott's "Introduction to the Study of the Gospels," another convenient and admirable manual.

bridge from the old economy to the new. John carries forward the piers toward that final heavenly economy of which he gives us a glimpse in the Apocalypse. In Matthew we have Jesus as the Messiah; in John as the Eternal Word. In Matthew He is the fulfilment of prophecy. In John He is Himself the prophet and the earnest of better, heavenly things to come. "His record is a creative source, and not a summary; the opening of a new field of thought, and not the gathered harvest." Matthew keeps Christ before us as the interpreter and fulfiller of the law: in John He appears introducing the grander and richer economy of the Spirit. In the one He satisfies the law, in the other the want of humanity. John represents Him as the world's life; the disciple's friend and teacher; the object of faith, the magnet of love, the focal point of prayer, the goal of hope, the inspirer of service. Matthew's backward look stops at Abraham; John leads us back into the eternal past, where dwelt the Word before Abraham was. In Matthew we have the new interpretation of old precept; in John, the fact and the secret of fellowship. Matthew tells how to follow Him, John how to abide in Him. Matthew's gospel is the gospel of an infant church, John's of a matured church.

Or take the parables. Sometimes it seems as if Christ were repeating Himself, or simply piling up illustration round a single truth. On the contrary, it will always be found that the truth is many-sided, and that the illustrations grow from the different sides. Three parables, for instance, are grouped round the topic of Christ's saving the lost : the Lost Sheep, the Lost Coin, and the Lost Son. The first two are an answer to the Pharisees, who complained that He ate with publicans and sinners, and who counted a common man of less value than a sheep. In the third, the explanation of His conduct is referred to its higher reason as the work of the Father. In the parable of the sheep, the interest centres in the loss : of the coin, in the search : of the son, in the restoration. In the first is pictured loss through stupid and blind straying : in the second, loss in the very sphere of the king-dom of God, through the power of worldly circumstance which withdraws the man from circulation, and obscures God's image in him, as the dust hides the superscription of the coin. In the third, loss through wilful aban-donment of filial privilege : so that we see loss under the three aspects of witlessness, useless-ness, and rebelliousness.— Once more, the seeker of the lost appears under the power of three motives: compassion for man's misery; a sense of the humblest man's transcendent value; and consummate fatherly love.

Or look at the two parables which set forth the lesson of faithful service:—The Talents and the Pounds. These are not the same. Luke does not put Matthew into another form. The lessons are different. Look at Luke. Ten servants: a pound to each servant: interest ten pounds for one: reward, ten cities, and "good servant." Interest five pounds for one; reward five cities, and no "good servant." In other words, endowment equal, interest unequal, standard of merit and of reward determined by amount or quantity; ten cities for ten per cent.; five cities for five per cent., with an unpleasant hint in the omission of "good servant." Now turn to Matthew. Three servants: five talents to one, two to another, one to the third. Interest five talents on five; reward, "Good and faithful servant, enter into the joy of thy Lord." Interest two talents on two. Reward, "Good and faithful servant, enter into the joy of thy Lord." Thus we have, endowment unequal, interest unequal, but reward equal: standard of merit and of reward determined not by quantity, but by quality. The same reward is assigned to different quantities because both bear the common stamp of faithfulness. In short, where servants equally endowed make an unequal use of their endowments, they are unequally rewarded. Where servants unequally endowed are equally faithful, the reward is equal.*

Take the " Beatitudes" at the opening of the Sermon on the Mount. Do you think that those blessings are thrown out at random, and that it would make no difference whether our Lord should begin with " Blessed are the poor in spirit," or " Blessed are they that are persecuted for righteousness' sake"? Not so indeed. This series is constructed on a definite plan, and proceeds with a close, inner, logical connection. Note first how the blessings fall into two groups, answering to the arrangement of both the Lord's Prayer and the Decalogue: the first four, like the first four commandments, and the first four items of the Lord's prayer, looking upward, from earth to heaven, from man to God, and indicating qualities in man as related to God: the other group looking earthward, and contemplating

---

* I would earnestly recommend teachers to procure and study Dr. A. B. Bruce's work on " The Parabolic Teaching of Christ." It is published by A. C. Armstrong & Son.

man's relations to his fellow-man, and to his
earthly surroundings.

Then, note further, a progress in the arrangement. The sermon starts from a point
outside the kingdom of God, and shows us
how a man comes into it. The blessings,
therefore, follow the steps of progress toward
citizenship. Our Lord brings the kingdom
of Heaven at once into the field of vision.
The man says, "What is the kingdom of
Heaven to me? Why should I want it?"
That is the very question. Are you conscious
of any reason why you should want it? Do
you feel any need of it? If not, you will not
gain it, for only those who feel such a need
seek and find it. Hence, "Blessed are the
poor in spirit" could properly stand nowhere
else than at the beginning. Poverty of spirit
means just what poverty means always and
everywhere. It means to the spiritual and
moral nature what being poor means to the
pocket, to the appetite, to the naked and
chilled body — conscious want: a sense of
emptiness. Spiritually, it is the opposite of
self-satisfaction; and no man will seek the
kingdom of God, of which the first principle
is "Deny self," so long as he is satisfied with
self.

When one has squarely confronted his need,

and has confessed to himself, "I am poverty-stricken at the very sources of my being," the result will be mourning. There will be something in him answering to the poor man's gnawing pain from hunger, and his chill from cold. Therefore mourning drops naturally into the second place. A Roman poet tells us how one of the gates of the city of Rome was always dropping moisture from its arches. It is a type of the entrance to the kingdom of Heaven, which is through tears. The sorrow is the sorrow of conscious mistake, of disappointment, of wounded pride, of newly discovered weakness and sinfulness: sorrow over emptiness of wisdom, of satisfaction, of cause for self-gratulation, of strength and of goodness.

The man who is really hungry and thirsty will take such food as you give him. The beggar is not the chooser. Sorrow accomplishes nothing until it brings us down to the point where we are ready, not only to accept and endorse God's charge of weakness and error, but to take His remedy for these, whatever it be: ready and willing to be fed with God's meat; to take God's prescription for sin; to take Christ's yoke of docility and submissive obedience. Here, therefore, Meekness, the spirit of absolute submission and subjection, grounded in a true humility, falls into its appropriate place.

From a sorrowful and often vague sense of need, and a meek willingness to confess its source and to have it supplied in God's own way and on God's own terms, we move on to the clearer definition of the need itself. The man finds out what he wants. All his sense of emptiness and his consequent mourning and submissiveness now run into the channel of one great desire—to be holy. He hungers and thirsts after righteousness. Christ says to him, " The thing you have all along wanted is *rightness;* right relation to me and to my law and to my children. Seek that first—my kingdom and my rightness." This desire is no sickly sentiment. Hunger and thirst mean vigorous appetite. Holiness is adapted to call out all the best energies. Our Lord and His apostles never contemplate any lower ideal than an enthusiasm in its pursuit. You see how naturally this beatitude falls into line with the others. Poverty of spirit engenders mourning; mourning, meekness; poverty, mourning, meekness, issue in holy desire, and desire in satisfaction. " They shall be filled."

Now we turn earthward. A man filled with God's righteousness, which includes joy and peace, can not keep it to himself. Righteousness is in him, not as dead precept, but as "a fountain of water springing up." Righteousness, like water in a reservoir, is pervaded with a thrust and pressure outward and downward toward men. It will get out of the man, and flow to his brethren in the form of mercy. The next blessing, as we might expect, is on the merciful. Mercy is rightness toward God , taking shape in loving rightness toward men. It grows out of righteousness as a branch from a vine. You find the same essential connection between righteousness and mercy in the Old Testament. Says the Psalmist, "Unto Thee, O Lord, belongeth mercy, for Thou renderest to every man according to his work." There is no clash between righteousness and mercy, as is so often assumed. It was the highest righteousness which gave the world the grandest token of mercy. It is the Just - who is the Justifier.

But here we are guarded. There is a something called mercy which has no essential connection with righteousness; but is merely a natural, humane impulse, a kindly "good-nature," which often finds expression in kind and helpful deeds, but which often goes hand in hand with unbridled self - indulgence. Righteousness is the test of mercy on the one side; now Christ puts a test on the other side :—Purity of heart ; righteousness at its fountain-head. Therefore we recognize the true place of the next beatitude, " Blessed are the pure in heart."

Then, for I must hasten on, a pure heart is a peaceful heart, because at peace with God ; and such a heart seeks to be at peace with men, and studies the things which make for peace. Notice that the blessing is not to peaceable men, but to *makers* of peace ; promoters of it among their brethren. It is the part of a righteous man not only to " keep the peace " himself, but to come, bringing Christ's olive-branch into the midst of their dissensions and strifes. This, then, is the true place for the blessing on the Peacemakers.

But to such an one, peace means, first of all, right. He knows no peace at the expense of right. Christ is the " Prince of peace,' but righteousness is the " girdle of his loins." Hence Christ's disciple inevitably comes into collision with an unrighteous world, and the result is persecution for righteousness' sake. The very lips which uttered this beatitude, said, " I came not to send peace, but a sword." This blessing rightly closes the list. It would be manifestly out of place at the beginning. It presupposes all that is contained in the preceding beatitudes.

So of the Lord's prayer. Put "Our Father which art in Heaven," anywhere but at the beginning, and see if you can pray that prayer. Begin, for instance, with "Thy kingdom come." What a tremendous question, what an awful doubt you encounter at once. "*Thy* kingdom"! But *whose* kingdom? What is it, or who is it that we are inviting to lay us under absolute subjection and tribute? Is it a beneficent power, or a power of evil and tyranny? The doubt is forestalled by the words "Our Father, *Thy* kingdom come." But not to dwell on the matter of order and progress in the Lord's prayer, note the miraculous way in which the whole Sermon on the Mount is packed into it. Take up that sermon at any point, and you will strike a line leading directly to the Lord's prayer. A heavenly economy of life must include some provision for putting and keeping us consciously in contact with Heaven. It must be an economy which we can pray as well as live. And therefore the Sermon on the Mount, which is the manual of the kingdom of Heaven, the exposition of the divine economy of life, has a prayer bedded in its heart, and connected by living fibres with its entire structure. The Lord's prayer is the Sermon on the Mount cast into aspiration.

I have only to remark farther, that Christ shows His consummate art as a teacher by His skilful veiling and draping of His lines of system. The fault of many teachers is in unduly emphasizing their plan. A Sunday-school lesson may be so ingeniously constructed as to draw all the attention to its structure, while its subject-matter goes begging; and many a preacher has spoiled a sermon by keeping the lines and joints of his plan constantly on the surface. Nature gives us a lesson on this point. She is the greatest of systematizers, with the widest range and the richest variety in her surface developments. She builds a man over a skeleton, but she hides the skeleton; and it is the flash of the eye, the mobility and variety of expression, the inflections of the voice, the infinite diversity of movement and attitude, which appeal to us, and not the nice articulation of bones. With Christ, method was a means and not an end. He aimed at direct contact of the heart with the living substance of His speech; and it was because nothing was suffered to stand between these, that men said, " Never man spake like this man."

CHRIST A GREAT QUESTIONER.

I have but a few minutes left for one other point. Christ was a great questioner.

It is a common saying that any fool may ask a question which a wise man can not answer. That is true; but it does not follow that any fool knows how to question. It requires quite as much wisdom to put questions as to answer them. Christ was early found in the temple asking questions; not indeed as a teacher, for a lecturing Christ-child would have been a monstrosity befitting the Apocryphal gospels rather than the narratives of the Evangelists. But those old Rabbis knew what apt questioning was, and they were astonished at the wisdom of His questions as well as of His answers. Socrates was a master of the art ; and it is the skilful, subtle questioning which leads on and sustains our interest through a dialogue of Plato. Paul deals much in interrogation. In the Epistle to the Romans, you will find six questions in the second chapter, sixteen in the third, six in the sixth, nine in the ninth, ten in the eleventh ; and so in other epistles. Christ's teaching abounds in question, and in question aimed at a great variety of ends. If you assume the teacher at your first contact with the uninstructed, you are quite as likely to excite his resentment as his interest or respect ; for ignorance is generally conceited, and it touches his conceit, not that you should know more than he does, but that you should assume to know more. If you make him a sharer in your thought by a question which appeals to his thought, you catch him on the side of his sympathy.

You will observe how often Christ introduces His lessons by a question, apparently very simple and commonplace, which draws the hearer's mind into His own train of thought and enlists his attention and interest before he knows it. "What think ye? If a man have an hundred sheep, and one go astray, doth he not leave the ninety and nine and go after the one?" "What think ye of the Christ? Whose son is he?" Or sometimes He tells a story, as He only knew how to tell it, and then a question puts the clew of the lesson into the hearer's hand, and sets him at following it up. "Which now of these three thinkest thou was neighbor to him that fell among thieves?" "The Lord frankly forgave both the debtors: Simon, which of the two will love Him most?" The question at the beginning has a power of arrest; at the end, a power of lodgment. Sometimes He combines the two, as in the story of the two sons sent into the vineyard: "What think ye?" and, at the end, "Whether of the twain did the will of his father?" Sometimes He uses a question to silence or to commit an adversary:

"The baptism of John, was it from heaven or of men?" or in the parable of the wicked husbandmen: "What shall therefore the Lord of the vineyard do?" Sometimes, again, to make a point on which to hang a lesson. "Those eighteen on whom the tower in Siloam fell,—suppose ye they were sinners above all that dwelt in Jerusalem? I tell you nay; but except ye repent, ye shall all likewise perish." Sometimes, to bring home a truth of God's love and tenderness by a familiar analogy. "If your son ask bread, will you give him a stone?" "If God clothe the grass, shall He not much more clothe you?" Or again, to bring an every-day truth over into the moral consciousness: "Do men gather grapes of thorns, or figs of thistles?" "Which of you, proposing to build a tower, does not first count the cost?" Or, once more, to bring out some conceit or delusion, as when, at the close of the series of parables in the thirteenth of Matthew, He asks, "Have ye understood all these things?" One is tempted to smile at the ready complacency with which they answered, "Yea, Lord!"

II.

At the conclusion of my lecture last year, you kindly requested me to discuss some other aspects of the same subject at which I hinted, but which I had not time to treat then. Resuming, therefore, the former theme, I shall speak first of

CHRIST AS A GREAT ILLUSTRATOR.

All great teachers have recognized the power of illustration. Plato revels in it. Dante's "Commedia" and Homer's "Iliad" and "Odyssey" are picture-books. The part of a sermon which sticks, is the illustrative part. Often the hearer will carry away nothing else. Dr. Beman, of Troy, used to say that if he wanted to preach an old sermon and not have it recognized (a very useless precaution, by the way), he *took out the bears;* meaning those striking illustrations which, being lodged in the hearers' memory, would serve to identify the sermon. Unless he put in some other "animals" of the same kind, I must needs say, with all reverence to his memory, that he was likely to purchase concealment at the expense of inter-

est. You can not teach children effectively
without illustration. You must appeal to the
eye; and that fact is recognized in the best
modern educational systems. And in the process of learning, the average man is not greatly
in advance of the child as respects this matter.
Not logic, but seeing, is the shortest way to
truth. Seeing is believing. Christ came, a
light into the world, that men might know
the truth. Most words are originally meta-
phors or picture-forms into which the primi-
tive man casts a statement. After a time the
lines of the picture fade, and the word be-
comes merely the symbol of a fact, yet it
always carries the original picture deep down
in its heart. It was something beside super-
stition which filled the old churches with
paintings and mosaics. Men can not always
read books, but they can read pictures. When
there were no books or few books, and reading
was confined to priests, they did the people a
Christian service who painted their Gospel for
them. So, when the worshipper could read
the story of the creative week on the choir-
walls of Monreale, or the stories of Abraham
and Sarah and Melchizedek behind the altar
of San Vitale at Ravenna, or could follow the
whole history of redemption in St. Mark's at
Venice, from the fall of man, and the lives of

the patriarchs in the portico, to the ascension
of Jesus in the overarching dome,—he was
not without a Bible. We forget sometimes
how much the painters helped to carry the
truth of the Gospel over the gap of the dark
ages.

Illustrations serve the same purpose, for
illustrations are pictures. The highest en-
dorsement of illustrative teaching is furnished
by Christ. Let us consider some of the char-
acteristics of this method as employed by
Him.

It is essential to a good illustration that it
should turn on a point common to the under-
standing of teacher and pupil alike. If I were
trying to teach an African savage a religious
truth by means of an illustration drawn from
the use of the telephone, I should only con-
fuse him, and give him two difficulties for one.
He does not know what a telephone is, to begin with. I could do it with an illustration
taken from his bow or canoe or war-club, for
both he and I know what those are and what
they mean.

You observe, therefore, that Christ's illustrations always start from a point as familiar
to His hearers as to Himself. If He had cited
some marvel of the spiritual world out of
which He came, some most ordinary feature

of His heavenly dwelling-place, they would
only have stared at Him, and their interest in
the truth He was expounding would have
given place to curiosity excited by this new
wonder. Instead of that, He takes a man
building a house, or finding treasure in a field,
or sowing seed, or catching fish, or a woman
sweeping the floor or making bread. He sets
the hearer on the familiar, commonplace truth,
so that from it he can reach up to the higher
and less familiar spiritual truth.

Hence our Lord drew a great many of His
illustrations from nature. All His hearers
knew how seed was sown and the stages by
which it grew. They were familiar with the
stony and the thorny ground and the hard-
beaten wayside. They were wont to watch
the changes of the sky, and they knew the
quick rising and the terrible sweep of the
mountain torrent. They had considered the
lilies, the sparrows, and the reed shaken with
the wind. Even the familiar aspects of nature,
however, never appeal to men so strongly as
when they are somehow associated with man's
person or work or danger or pleasure : and
therefore, in Christ's illustrations from nature,
He draws largely on its aspects after it has
felt the hand of man. He takes His hearers
to the vineyard, but the husbandman is there,

tending and pruning the vines. To the field,
but the sower comes, scattering seed by the
wayside and among the thorns. He bids
them mark the sparrows, but they are the
dead sparrows, strung on spits, and sold in
the market. He tells of the flocks, but the
prominent figure is the good shepherd ; of
the mountain torrent, but as it sweeps away
the foolish man's house from its sandy foun-
dation.

The significance of this feature of Christ's
illustrative teaching is too large a subject to
be discussed here, but the theme is, neverthe-
less, too tempting to be dismissed without a
few words. This habitual association of nature with man furnishes more than a hint of
the depth of Christ's insight into nature, and
of the comprehensiveness and symmetry of
His view of the universe ; for it reveals His
recognition of the fact that nature finds its .
chief significance and its highest interpretation in man. Nature, even on the physical
side, does not give up its best to the bird or
the beast. The jungle, however luxuriant,
can never mean nor yield so much as the field
of sown corn. But, in its association with
man, nature yields more than food or building material. It furnishes spiritual and moral
lessons which have no meaning and no appli-

cation apart from man, and which only man can receive and appropriate. The whole spiritual meaning of nature lies latent until nature is touched by man. And this meaning our Lord is at pains that men should extract from it. He would have them know that this relation between man and nature enables him to make even brute bulks and familiar physical forces vocal with truths of the soul. He is not satisfied that they should draw from nature only bread and drink and impressions of form and color; and accordingly he lifts nature into the seat of a spiritual teacher. The corn of wheat, casting its seed-form and taking on the nobler vesture of the full corn in the ear, in some valley unvisited by man, means only a few grains for the bird or a mouthful for the browsing beast. When man comes, only then, Christ comes and makes that dying and risen wheat-corn a lesson and a type of death unto self, spiritual resurrection, and moral fruitfulness.

Paul, though surely not blind to this truth, does not work it into his teaching as Christ does. In his Epistles we breathe chiefly "the air of cities and synagogues." He draws very sparingly on Nature for illustration, and manifestly lacks that quick and exquisite susceptibility to the various phases of nature which so strongly marks our Lord. Yet there is, even at this point, a deep-lying resemblance between them, in that both see "the universe of God as it is reflected in the heart and life of man." No one can help feeling this in reading Paul's words in the eighth of Romans, on the "groan and travail" of the creation— the sympathy of man's material and animal environment with the pangs and longings of fallen humanity.*

From his habit of selecting familiar things for illustrations, we are quite prepared to find his range of illustration extending into the domestic and business spheres. Men are familiar most of all with their homes. Therefore we are pointed to the grain-measure which was in every house, together with the lamp-stand and the bed. The woman loses her silver in the house, and lights her lamp

---

* I can not but think that Canon Farrar ("Life and Work of St. Paul," I., 18-21) is rather too sweeping in his assertion that Paul "reveals not the smallest susceptibility for the works of nature." I fear I must have failed to apprehend his meaning, where he says that the illustration of the wild-olive graft (Rom. xi. 16-25) is "the only elaborate illustration which Paul draws from nature"; for it seems inconceivable that the Canon should have overlooked the fifteenth of First Corinthians. Indeed he cites the allusion to the stars in v. 41.

and sweeps. The home-life is the background of the story of the prodigal. There is the wedding feast, and the servant sitting up for his master; the boy asking his father for a cake of bread; the washing of the dishes, and the rich man building new barns. The conceited guest enters and takes the first place at the banquet; the woman sets her bread to rise, or grinds at the handmill; the scoundrel sows darnel by night among the wheat, and the belated traveller knocks at midnight at his neighbor's door, and asks for a loaf of bread. The pictures are from the market and the street also; sometimes flashing out from a single word. "Good measure shall men give *into your bosom"*; a dark saying to the man who goes to Washington market with his basket on his arm, but not so to the oriental, into the loose bosom of whose robe the trader would pour the day's supply of grain. The servants are away with their pounds to the money-changers; the steward bustles about among his lord's creditors and discounts their bills for cash; the creditor chokes his debtor on the highway, and the widow pleads her cause before the judge in the gate. In our Lord's teaching, moreover, the illustration is invariably subordinate to the truth illustrated, and grows naturally out of it.

Unlike some modern teachers, He does not first light on His illustration and then trim and mould the truth to fit it. There are no stained windows in the structure of Christ's discourse, to stay the eye on themselves. The illustrations are for letting in light upon the truth. You can easily see that the great theme of the relations of men's souls to truth and their attitude toward God's Word, suggests the illustration of the seed on different soils, and that the process is not the contrary one. You can easily see that the grand conception of the pervasion of society with the spirit and law of God, came, in Christ's mind, before the picture of the woman hiding the leaven. The greater suggested the less. The illustration does not dominate the truth nor distract the attention from the truth to itself. Some teachers pour forth such a bewildering variety of brilliant illustration that the pupil loses sight of the truth altogether. Not a few modern sermons have had their genesis in a telling anecdote or a striking figure, and the whole sermon has been one ingenious inquisitorial process of stretching a truth upon the rack of that pet illustration.

But with all the simplicity of Christ's illustrations, they have an enormous range. On the surface they sometimes appear to explain merely the fragment of truth thrown out by the great teacher at the moment; but the fragment, on examination, reveals connections with a large area of truth, and the illustration is found to cover the entire area no less than the fragment. Take, for instance, the familiar parable of the talents, and the Lord's comment. "To him that hath shall be given, from him that hath not shall be taken away." That truth ranges over the whole physical, intellectual, and spiritual life of men. The old woman who sells peanuts on the corner knows perfectly that she must have something to buy her peanuts with, before she can realize a profit on them. She and the capitalist are alike in that. Nothing is given to either of them without their first having. The man who has, makes. The educated and trained man masters a subject or does a piece of intellectual work better and more quickly than the untrained man of equal native ability. He wins the new knowledge through the disciplined power which he has. An artist draws more inspiration and more ideas in a day from a beautiful landscape than the ignorant cow-feeder who has passed his whole life amid its beauties. Nature gives to the mind which has. The man who has power of any kind is in a position to gain more power. In short, the truth holds all the way up, that capital brings interest. It holds in religion as else-where. The same words—"To him that hath shall be given"—are added to the parable of the sower. The stress is laid, in that parable, not on the seed, which is assumed to be good, but on the soil. Where the soil had the right quality with which to meet the seed, there was fruit; though there was a difference in the fruitfulness of even the good soil, represented by thirty, sixty, and a hundred. The interest of Gospel truth and power presupposes the possession of an honest and good heart in the recipient.

You can follow out the same line of thought with the parables of the Mustard-seed and the Leaven. Or take Christ's illustration of the corn of wheat. How far-reaching is the truth it carries; that a higher form of life is always won at the expense of a lower; that the highest life comes through death; that all success costs. The business-man succeeds at the price of literary leisure and culture; the boy grows into a man of learning and thought through the partial suppression of his animal instinct to play; a man and woman attain in marriage that joint life of love, of higher quality than the separate individuality of either, through the partial merging of each individuality. Christ's sharp alternative is, the world or the soul. The soul is won at the price of the world. The sensual life must go under if the higher life of faith and love is to come to fruitage. So you see that the illustration, beginning in agriculture, covers business and learning and domestic life and religion.

CHRIST A GREAT NARRATOR.

But leaving this vein of thought, let us explore another lying close beside it. Christ was a great narrator. It is a great art to be able to tell a story well, for it is an art which appeals to all mankind. In all times and countries men have welcomed the story-teller. We are all children in this. It does not show that a man is becoming wiser because he is losing his taste for stories. The child and the old man meet here on common ground. It is one of the harmless foibles of old age that it repeats its old stories. Charles Lamb somewhere tells of a man who had retired, in a green old age, upon forty pounds a year and one anecdote. The great successes in literature have been largely stories. " Robinson Crusoe," " The Pilgrim's Progress," and " The Arabian Nights," are treasures forever. Homer's " Odyssey" will always have more readers than the "Iliad." Froissart will be well thumbed, while Hume and Lingard gather dust on the shelves. Macaulay will never lack readers, because he has imparted to English History the fascination of a story; and Herodotus will continue to hold his own among the more modern magnates of history. In any circulating library they will tell you that the demand for novels exceeds threefold that for any other class of books. Ten thousand of "Helen's Babies," and "Barriers Burned Away," are sold for one thousand of the best essays or sermons in the language. Very few people now living have read, I imagine, Goldsmith's "Animated Nature," but who has not read "The Vicar of Wakefield"? The Bible has made its way to the people largely by its stories.— The boy of fifteen knows nothing about the Epistle to the Romans, but he can tell you all about Joseph and Moses and Samson.

Story-telling, I repeat, is an art, and a fine art. It seems as though it might be an easy thing to write a story like "Robinson Crusoe," but try it once. And there are certain features which, you notice, are common to all good story-tellers. Their first object, for instance, is to tell the story. A good many writers attempt stories as a kind of staging for their moral reflections; and, if the story has any interest at all, you usually find that the staging occupies the reader so that he overlooks the building. In other words, he skips the moral reflections and hurries on along the line of the story. Again, all good stories run. Chaucer's "Canterbury Tales," "Robinson Crusoe," "The Arabian Nights," are full of movement; and the writers of popular fiction are coming to recognize that fact, and to shape their productions accordingly. The popular romance of the day is not the old three-volume novel, but the short story with a simple plot and a succession of incidents gathering up rapidly to a climax.

Our Lord was a great master of narrative, and His stories exhibit not only the two qualties of which we have been speaking, but others which we shall note later. The best way to illustrate this is to examine one of His stories in detail; and we can not hesitate in the choice of a specimen, for the story of the Prodigal Son is the model story of all literature, both as to contents and method.

Observe, then, that Christ goes straight at the story. He does not work up to it through any elaborate introduction or learned prelude. We have no long family history of this good old father. "A certain man"—no matter who or whence, any man will answer—"had two sons." There is no display of the narrator's power of analyzing character fastened upon a description of these two sons. All that the reader needs to know about them is left to come out in the development of the story itself.

Then follows the fact out of which the plot of the story grows. Here, too, the reader is left to infer for himself the motives and feelings of the younger son—what he had been secretly brooding over; what hopes and ambitions he had been fostering; the whole process by which he had worked up to his decisive, unfilial act—all, in short, which would have furnished a chapter to the modern philosophical romancer. The young man is introduced in the very act of striking the blow which cuts him loose from father and from home. A thoughtful reader will gather a great deal from those few words, as Christ meant that he should. The ingratitude, the insolence of the demand for his portion of goods, the insensibility to the privilege and love and protection of home—all are there, but wrapped up in the simple statement of his wicked act. Here the modern dramatic story-teller would have discovered another great opportunity. I have somewhere seen this part of the narrative

worked up; how the old man, when the boy
came into his presence, was seated at a table
counting out, with trembling hands, a great
pile of gold and silver, and more to the same
effect. Now there is no pause. " Not long
after." Every sentence tells. The youth
wanted to manage his own affairs absolutely.
He would leave nothing in his father's hands.
" He gathered *all* together, and *straightway*
took his journey," and went as far away as
he could, "into a far country," out of reach
of fatherly hearing and counsel. And now
the modern prurient story-teller would find
his chance for a salacious description of a
luxurious and licentious life. That is one of
the favorite devices of the devils of modern
literature. It is needless to remark how pure
Christ's stories are. He uses the plainest words
where there is occasion, but He never pictures
sin so as to make it otherwise than ugly.

Short and sharp again, but how vivid.
" Scattered " is the word used of winnowing the
grain. "He scattered his substance, living un-
savingly." The great truth that absence from
God is waste of life was never more tersely put:
a far country and waste. We move on at once to
the consequence. When the famine came, he
had nothing. " He had spent *all*." Moral waste
is total waste. " He began to be in want."

The painful and sometimes amusing adventures of reduced men in search of employment have furnished many a good story; but how powerfully that whole stage of the prodigal's career is put by the use of a single peculiar word, " he *joined himself* to a citizen." The word means to "glue " or "stick to "; and its use here seems to imply that the swine-owner was not over-eager to employ him. In time of famine people dispense with as many servants as possible ; and it would seem as though the penniless young wanton had to force himself upon the citizen. And so this swine-capitalist, having nothing else for him to do, or possibly with a vulgar satisfaction at having a decayed gentleman at his mercy, sent him into the fields to feed swine. Here the realistic story-teller would disport himself with the unsavory details of swine-keeping, and would draw out the contrast with the luxurious halls of pleasure. Nothing of this. The one thought to be driven home at this point is *want*. You see what a quick succession and sharp putting of points there is: conceit and insubordination: waste: want. One or two sentences have furnished the world a synonym for soul - hunger. " He would fain have filled his belly with the husks which the swine did eat, and no man gave

unto him." He had wanted the wrong thing
all along, and it was no better now. All he
wanted was to fill his belly. Suffering had
not yet issued in longing for better things.

Now another point: " He came to himself."
Let your plummet down into that sentence,
and you will find it very deep. It opens into
the great truth that rebellion against God is a
kind of madness. Man is his true self only
when he is a loyal son in God's household: a
madman else—in a delirious dream. What a
stroke of art in representing the beginning of
repentance as the return of a sound consciousness. And a chapter of imaginary, doleful
reflections and contrasts could not exhibit the
prodigal's awakened thought so graphically as
this one sharp contrast in which he voices it.
" My father's house—the very servants there
have bread enough and to spare, and I, his
own son, am perishing with hunger!"

Now reflection merges into resolution. " I
will arise! I will go home! I will confess
my sin!" No description now of the scenery
along the road, nor of the various adventures
encountered on the journey; tricks of the
story-teller to sharpen the reader's appetite
for the climax by keeping him in suspense.
The narrator is full of the thought of home,
just as the reader is. At this point of the

story you feel just as you do when you are returning to your native town and family homestead after years of absence. You do not care a penny for all the scenery in the world. The most exciting incident on the way is insipid. You only chafe at the delay it creates. You want to hurry those horses; to pull out the throttle-valve of that engine, and drive through to home. Neither does the narrator stop while he affectingly pictures the old father looking out of the window or scanning the road, and tell of the tears with which he has moistened his pillow in the lonely nights when the rain was on the roof. The story needs no such details to make it pathetic. Its pathos lies deeper. Home, home is the theme. It is all in a sentence. "He arose and went to his father." Pathos! In following such a story as this, one can weep as he runs. I wonder if any one can go on from this point without the floods pressing to his eyes. Oh, how the blessed details crowd upon each other. Swiftly as the story moved at the beginning, its pace quickens as it gathers up for the close. The father sees, — sees him a great way off. All the past looking and yearning are in that. Love and longing have made him far-sighted. "He ran." Love never lets its object come the whole way. Divine love urges the sinner to come, but it goes to meet him. Every feeling is now swallowed up in compassion. The embrace is first from the father's side. He falls on his son's neck. The confession is breathed, but without the request to be made a hired servant. The boy never could have said that with those arms round his neck.

And now we reach the climax. Festivity. The joyful bustle of the awakened house has gotten into the story. How the orders pour from the happy father. " My son is at home with a son's heart in him. Bring out the best robe for him. My son is no dishonored beggar, but an honored guest. Put a ring on his finger. It is not fitting that my son should be hungry. Bring forth the fatted calf and kill it. The shadow is lifted from this home. Let us eat and drink and be merry,—servants and all." And then comes the whole Gospel in a brief paragraph. Man is a son of God: he is lost and dies by absence from God: he is found and lives again by penitent return to God. " This my son was dead and is alive again, he was lost and is found."

I may take occasion here to remark that while enlargement upon the hints furnished by Scripture narratives is legitimate and often profitable, it is not that easy matter which it

often seems to a lively and teeming fancy;
and to do it effectively is something which requires nice judgment and a very clear insight
into the whole drift and spirit of the story. A
danger lies close beside it, of covering up the
best points of the narrative with excessive or
incongruous description, and of making it
ridiculous by importing into it things quite
alien to its meaning and original setting. I
once heard a preacher describing the conver-
sion of Saul of Tarsus. He brought him to
Damascus, and then proceeded on this wise:
"When Saul arrived at Damascus, he went at
once to his hotel in Straight Street, and went
directly to his room. To most people, the
most pleasing sound in the world is the sound
of the dinner-bell; but *when the dinner-bell
rang, Saul didn't go down!*" And I found
the following morsel in a volume of sermons
for children, where the preacher was telling
the story of Zacharias, the father of John the
Baptist. He described Zacharias' recovery of
speech as follows. I quote literally: "And
while they were all wondering what this
meant, *old Zacharias gave a rattling kind of
gurgle in his throat, or coughed away something
that had been like a heavy cold on him,* and he
who had not spoken a word for nine months,
now spoke out loudly like the rest of the peo-

ple and praised God." I think I shall not be deemed uncharitable in expressing the wish that Zacharias' enforced silence might be imposed, for a season at least, upon those who thus caricature the simple and dignified narratives of the Gospel, and feed the lambs of the flock with such miserable, I had almost said blasphemous trash.

Let me briefly note some other peculiarities of our Lord's narrative style, at some of which I have already hinted in the story of the Prodigal.

There is the dramatic element. Every good story contains more or less of this. There is a difference between annals and stories. Merely to string a number of incidents together is not to tell a story. Much of the effect of a story depends on the grouping of the incidents; the setting of the telling points in strong light and duly subordinating minor details. The art of story-telling consists in reproducing its scenes to the eye through the ear. The oriental story-teller and the *raconteur* of Southern Europe are actors. If you want a good modern illustration of how a story can be dramatized in narrative, you will find one in Charles Reade's charming little tale of " Christie Johnstone," where Christie tells to a holiday party of fishermen and fish-

wives the story of the "Merchant of Venice,"
as dramatized by Shakespeare. It is this
characteristic of the Gospel stories which makes
them such capital subjects for pictures; a fact
which the old artists who painted Scripture
scenes far more than their modern successors,
were not slow to appreciate. I should like to
say some things, if time permitted, about the
Bible stories in art; and to show you how
they adapt themselves to the various local peculiarities in which artists of different countries and times set them, without sacrificing
the point of their lessons. I will give you
just one instance. In the gallery of the
Louvre at Paris, there is a picture of the Prodigal Son by the younger Teniers, in which all
the details are distinctively Dutch. The
young man, in the costume of a Dutch gal-
lant, sits with two female companions at a table in front of an inn, on the shutter of which
a tavern-score is chalked, and holds out his
glass to be filled by an attendant. Over in
the right-hand corner appears a pigsty, where
a stable-boy is feeding the swine, but with his
head turned toward the table as if in envy of
the gay revellers there. The picture, with all
its unbiblical setting, yet tells the Bible story
effectively. Sensuality is the same under any
garb. The difference between the youth at

the table and the youth at the sty is only superficial. Degradation is only the lower and grosser side of sin, a truth in Holland as in Palestine. The possible swineherd is already in the gay prodigal.

You note the same dramatic element in the parable of the ten virgins. How vivid the long waiting; the heads bowed in slumber; the thrill of the midnight cry, "Behold the bridegroom!" the hurried filling and trimming of the lamps; the woful plaint, "Our lamps are going out!" the rush to the oil-vender; the closed door, and the stern finality of the terrible words from within, "I know you not!" Perhaps one of the most fearfully dramatic narratives of the New Testament is not always recognized as such, because of its brevity. I mean that of the rich man who would pull down his barns and build greater. With the most consummate art we are carried along in the current of the rich man's thought, forgetting with him everything but the heaps of treasure, the plans for the new barns, and the dreams of future luxury; when, like thunder from a clear sky, breaks "Thou fool! This night thy soul shall be required of thee!" And as at the sudden shifting of a scene, a whole unsuspected economy of life is disclosed, and with the rich fool, unconscious till this in-

stant of anything but money and barns, we
look into a realm where only the soul counts,
and riches count for nothing.

Included in this dramatic element is the fre-
quent use of dialogue. The characters speak
for themselves. This is characteristic of the
second part of the parable of the prodigal,
where the respectable son is introduced. No
disquisition on the unfilial, servile spirit which
sometimes accompanies "good and regular
standing," could be half so telling as the
glimpse we get of it at the house door, where
it comes out that the older son's highest conception of filial service is something to be
paid for with a feast. You will readily recall
similar instances, such as the story of the
wedding-feast, with the excuses of the several
people invited, and the closing incident of the
guest without the wedding-garment; also the
Talents, the Unrighteous Steward, and the
Laborers in the Vineyard. In these the characters interchange the appropriate language
of the field, the market, or the guest-chamber.

Just a word on the element of *verisimilitude*
already touched upon in discussing Christ's
illustrations. It might not be safe to assert too
positively that all these stories told by our
Lord are imagined. More than one of them
may be a narrative of something which had

actually fallen under the Master's observation. But, however that may be, every incident, every word, every detail of these stories might have been true.—Many of them, most indeed, have a local coloring which always arrests attention. It added to the effect of the parable of the Good Samaritan, for instance, that the scene was laid on the Jericho road, which, as everybody knew, was infested with thieves; while the passing of the priest and Levite would be emphasized by the equally familiar fact that Jericho was an important station of priests. Christ never employed an impossible or an improbable incident, and never took it out of its appropriate setting. And, therefore, in our teaching, it is always the safer course to reproduce these incidents as nearly as possible with their original circumstances; to see, and to try and make the learner see with Eastern eyes. It is hazardous to modernize a Bible story. The lesson may indeed assert itself through its incongruous setting, as we have seen in the case of the old painters; but something is likely to get into it which mars its beauty and blurs its perfect impression. After reading John's account of the marriage at Cana, one does not feel that our Lord is at home in Veronese's magnificent canvas, among the gorgeous robes

of Venetian courtiers and the costly para-
phernalia of an Italian banquet.

Wondrous teacher! How lucid His teaching, as with the brightness which cometh out
of the North, yet what depths in the heart of
the light! How terribly plain, yet how kindly.
How positive and dogmatic, yet how sweetly
reasonable. How profound and yet how simple. How vivid and graphic, yet how dignified. How outspoken, yet how pure. How
quick and subtle His perception of error or
sophistry, yet how frank and generous His
recognition of the smallest grain of truth.
How patient He is with ignorance; how gen-
tle with slowness of faith. How informal and
familiar His lessons, yet with what logical com-
pactness and system underneath them. How
strongly drawn the lines of truth, yet what a
freshness and freedom pervades it. What
a divinity breathes through all His words.
Surely, as we study, we shall find admiration
merging into worship, and our lips and hearts
giving back His own words—" Yea, Master,
Thou art indeed both Teacher and Lord; the
wisest, the best, the dearest of Teachers, because Lord over all, and blessed forever."